You Bet Your Britches, Claude

Story by Joan Lowery Nixon
Pictures by Tracey Campbell Pearson

Viking Kestrel

RAP　　226　9621 ✓

VIKING KESTREL

Published by the Penguin Group

Viking Penguin Inc., 40 West 23rd Street, New York, New York 10010, U.S.A.

Penguin Books Ltd, 27 Wrights Lane, London W8 5TZ, England

Penguin Books Australia Ltd, Ringwood, Victoria, Australia

Penguin Books Canada Ltd, 2801 John Street, Markham, Ontario, Canada L3R 1B4

Penguin Books (N.Z.) Ltd, 182–190 Wairau Road, Auckland 10, New Zealand

Penguin Books Ltd, Registered Offices: Harmondsworth, Middlesex, England

First published in 1989 by Viking Penguin Inc.
Published simultaneously in Canada

1　3　5　7　9　10　8　6　4　2

Text copyright © Joan Lowery Nixon, 1989
Illustrations copyright © Tracey Campbell Pearson, 1989
All rights reserved

LIBRARY OF CONGRESS CATALOGING IN PUBLICATION DATA

Nixon, Joan Lowery. You bet your britches, Claude / by Joan Lowery Nixon;
illustrated by Tracey Campbell Pearson.　p.　cm.
Summary: Shirley and Claude lead a settled life with their adopted
son, Tom, until Shirley goes to town to retrieve Tom's sister,
Bessie, and the two run into more than their share of trouble with criminals.
ISBN 0-670-82310-4　　[1. Frontier and pioneer life—Fiction.　2. Humorous stories.]
I. Pearson, Tracey Campbell, ill.　II. Title.
PZ7.N65Yo　1989
[E]—dc19　　88-38847

Color Separations by Imago Ltd., Hong Kong

Set in Cheltenham Book.

With love to Andrew Thomas Quinlan
J.L.N.

For Robby, Stevie and Ricky
T.C.P.

CHAPTER ONE

It was early in the morning, with the sun as yellow and hot as the yolk of a just-fried egg, when Shirley, Claude, and their newly adopted son Tom arrived in town.

"There's too many people around here to suit me," Claude said. "I'm hankerin' to get back home and settle into some peace and quiet." He shook his head sadly. "Only lately we ain't had us much peace and quiet."

He hitched the pair of sway-backed horses to a post and added, "I'd be happier than a pig in a mud puddle if I could keep away all those wrong-minded folks who come by our farm."

Shirley patted Claude's shoulder. "I'll think of somethin'," she said. "We can head for home soon as I pick up a few things for Tom and collect my reward money for catchin' the bank robber."

"You get busy with the shoppin'," Claude said. "I'll find the sheriff and bring him back here."

The minute Claude was gone, Tom led Shirley across the street and into *The Good Eats Cafe* where his sister Bessie had been left with Mrs. Krumbly.

The only customers were a pair of cowboys who were chewing hard on what looked like beef stew. A little cinnamon-haired girl, not much bigger than a spring cricket, was on her hands and knees scrubbing the floor.

"Bessie!" Tom called.

Bessie threw the scrub brush into the air and leaped up to hug Tom.

"Tom!" she yelled. "Where'd you go? Whatcha doin' here? Who's that you're with?"

"Bessie," Tom said, soon as he'd managed to pry her loose, "meet Shirley, who's so kind and tenderhearted that she's goin' to be our new mother."

"Oh no, she's not!" Mrs. Krumbly waddled out from the kitchen waving a big, drippy, stirrin' spoon. "That saucy, little, no-account, ragamuffin gal belongs to me!"

Well, Shirley never could stand to hear folks talk ugly, so she stepped up to Mrs. Krumbly, nose to nose, and said, "You got no call to bad-mouth Bessie. I'll pay you fair and square the twenty dollars you gave for her, but there's no two ways about it. Bessie is comin' with me."

Mrs. Krumbly made a grab for Bessie, but Bessie scooted around the scrub pail, sloshing water in Mrs. Krumbly's path. Mrs. Krumbly slipped and landed in the scrub pail where she stuck, kicking and waving her arms and legs like a beetle on its back.

"If anybody's gonna square things, it ought to be Mrs. Krumbly," Bessie shouted. "She's been hornswoggling her customers. First off, I spied her not givin' 'em enough change."

"Bessie's always had sharp eyes," Tom said.

"And second," Bessie went on, "that so-called beef stew she makes has more little critters in it than beef."

The two cowboys leaped up from their chairs grabbing their throats and making terrible noises.

Just then Claude and the sheriff walked in.

Claude thought on what he saw. Then he said, "Shirley, you want to tell me how come those cowboys are hoppin' around like frogs on a hot rock and that cook lady is sittin' in a scrub pail?"

"*I'll* tell you! I'll tell you everything that happened," Bessie said eagerly. "It's a long story."

But before Bessie could say a single word, Shirley hushed her. "You bet your britches, Claude!" she said.

CHAPTER TWO

The sheriff gave Shirley the fifty-dollar reward money for catching the bank robber. Before he took Mrs. Krumbly to jail he smiled at Bessie and said, "Little gal, you're as good as any legal, sworn-in deputy."

Shirley explained to Claude about Bessie, but Claude said, "Sister or no sister, there's no way to have peace and quiet with a chatty little eight-year-old gal in the house. You better find someone else to take her in, while I tend to the horses."

Shirley took Bessie in one hand and Tom in the other and headed to *Dandee's Dry Goods Store.* "First thing we're goin' to do is get some new clothes," Shirley said.

"But what's goin' to happen to Bessie?" Tom asked.

"Don't worry," Shirley said as they entered the store. "I'll think of somethin'."

Shirley bought Tom and Bessie each some shoes, striped suspenders for Tom, and a blue hairbow for Bessie. But all the while Bessie kept eyeing a tall, dusty cowboy who wandered through the store, his flat, empty saddlebags slung over his shoulder.

"I'll be with you soon," Mr. Dandee told the cowboy.

"No hurry," the cowboy said. "I'll just look around."

Shirley picked out underclothes and nightshirts, a petticoat for Bessie, a felt hat for Tom, and two cents worth of jellybeans. Then she asked to see some bolts of sturdy cotton.

"I'll be with you soon," Mr. Dandee called to the cowboy, who was at the back of the store.

"No hurry," the cowboy called back.

For Tom, Shirley picked out some dark brown twill that would wear well, and for Bessie, some soft blue cotton lawn just right for a cinnamon-haired little girl.

As Mr. Dandee began to measure out the goods, the cowboy hurried to the counter and laid down some change. "All I'm gettin' is this chawin' tobacco," he said and quick-like started toward the door.

But all of a sudden Bessie was in his way. She tugged at his bulging saddlebags and yelled for Shirley.

"Look out, you little nuisance!" the cowboy shouted.

Well, Shirley never could stand to hear folks talk ugly, so she stepped right up to the cowboy, nose to nose, and said, "You got no call to bad-mouth Bessie."

At that moment Bessie gave such a yank to the cowboy's saddlebags it pulled him off balance. Down he went, his saddlebags spilling out all the things he'd stolen from the store. A pair of red longjohns lay stretched out across him.

Shirley rested a foot on the cowboy's stomach, in the middle of the red longjohns, just in case he had a mistaken notion to move, while Mr. Dandee ran to find the sheriff.

Bessie shouted, "I spied that cowboy sneakin' all sorts of things into his saddlebags!"

"Bessie's always had sharp eyes," Tom said.

Just then Mr. Dandee, Claude, and the sheriff hurried into the store.

Claude thought on what he saw. Then he said, "Shirley, you want to tell me how come you stepped so hard on that man that he shot right out of his underwear?"

"*I'll* tell you! I'll tell you everything that happened," Bessie said eagerly. "It's a long, *long* story."

But before Bessie could say a single word, Shirley hushed her. "You bet your britches, Claude!" she said.

CHAPTER THREE

"Little gal, you're as good as any legal, sworn-in deputy," the sheriff told Bessie before he took the cowboy off to jail.

Shirley put an arm around Bessie's shoulders and said, "Claude, let's talk about keepin' Bessie."

"Nope," Claude said. "There's no way to have peace and quiet with a chatty little gal in the house."

Shirley handed some money to Mr. Dandee and said to Claude, "If you'll tote my parcels to the wagon, I'll take the rest of my reward money to the bank for safe keeping."

She took Bessie in one hand and Tom in the other and hurried down the street to the bank.

"What's goin' to happen to Bessie?" Tom asked.

"Don't worry," Shirley said. "I'll think of somethin'."

Nobody but Mr. Pilly, the cashier, was in the bank, so Shirley went straight to the customer window. Tom stood polite-like off to one side, but Bessie clambered up to peer through the iron grille on top of the counter.

Mr. Pilly quickly snapped shut a large, black satchel and scowled at Shirley. "I've got no time for you now," he said. "I've got to catch the next stage."

"But I want to put my money in the bank," Shirley said. "Where's Mr. Witherspoon, the bank president?"

"He's home in bed," Mr. Pilly said. "How much money do you want to put in the bank?"

"Thirty dollars," Shirley said.

Mr. Pilly smiled the way a hungry rattlesnake smiles at a prairie dog and scribbled something on a piece of paper. "In that case, give me your money. Here's your receipt." He snatched the bills, picked up his satchel, and strode to the door.

But all of a sudden Bessie was in his way. She tugged at his satchel and yelled for Shirley.

Mr. Pilly tugged back, shouting at Bessie. "Get out of my way, you little raggletaggle, trouble-making pest!"

Well, Shirley never could stand to hear folks talk ugly, so she stepped right up to Mr. Pilly, nose to nose, and said, "You got no call to bad-mouth Bessie."

Bessie gave such a yank to Mr. Pilly's satchel that he tumbled end over end down the steps, pulling Shirley, Bessie, and the satchel with him.

Mr. Pilly landed face down with Shirley sitting on top of him. The satchel broke open, spilling money into Shirley's lap.

Bessie leaped to her feet and shouted, "I spied what was in that satchel afore Mr. Pilly closed it, and I figured he was fixin' to steal it!"

"Bessie's always had sharp eyes," Tom said.

Folks crowded around to see what was making such a commotion, and Claude and the sheriff came running.

Claude thought on what he saw. Then he said, "Shirley, you want to tell me how come you're sittin' on the bank cashier, countin' his money?"

"*I'll* tell you. I'll tell you everything that happened," Bessie said eagerly. "It's a long, long, *long* story."

But Shirley hushed her. She got up and said to the sheriff, "You said yourself that Bessie's as good as any legal, sworn-in deputy."

"Better," the sheriff said. "In all my days I've never seen anyone so quick at catchin' crooks."

"So why not make her a real, legal, sworn-in deputy?" Shirley asked.

The sheriff studied on it. "She's a mite young and small to be a deputy," he said.

"Look at it this way," Shirley said. "She can grow into the job."

"I guess that's right," the sheriff said. He took a tin star from his pocket and pinned it onto Bessie's dress. "Raise your right hand," he said.

As Bessie did, the sheriff, in a deep official-sounding voice said, "Under the rights given to me by the great state of Texas I hereby appoint this little gal Bessie an honest-to-goodness, everythin'-legal, sworn-in deputy. Bessie, you got somethin' to say in honor of the occasion?"

Bessie drew herself up as tall as she could and took a deep breath. "I'm right proud to be a deputy," she began.

But Shirley hushed her. "If we had a deputy livin' on our place," Shirley said to Claude, "the word would get out, and wrong-minded folks would steer clear."

"Makes sense to me," the sheriff said.

"And with no wrong-minded folks stoppin' by, our home would be mighty peaceful and quiet," Shirley said.

"Bound to be," the sheriff said.

Claude thought on it a moment. Then he smiled and said to Bessie, "Get in the wagon, daughter."

He took Shirley's arm. "No reason why we can't build *two* extra rooms onto the side of the house," he told her.

Shirley's smile was so bright that some folks around those parts got up and pulled down their window shades. She took Bessie's hand and held it tightly. "You bet your britches, Claude!" she said.